W9-CIE-935

DON'T CALL ME PRUNEFACE!

Written by
Janet Reed Ahearn

illustrated by
Drazen Kozjan

Disney • Hyperion Books
New York

To Dan, for making everything possible —J.R.A.

To Janet, Holly & Emily —D.K.

Text copyright © 2010 by Janet Reed Ahearn
Illustrations copyright © 2010 by Drazen Kozjan

All rights reserved. Published by Disney • Hyperion Books, an imprint of Disney Book Group. No part of this book may be reproduced or transmitted in any form or by any means, electronic or mechanical, including photocopying, recording, or by any information storage and retrieval system, without written permission from the publisher.
For information address Disney • Hyperion Books, 114 Fifth Avenue, New York, New York 10011-5690.

First Edition
10 9 8 7 6 5 4 3 2 1

F850-6835-5-10105

Reinforced binding
Printed in Singapore

ISBN 978-1-4231-1918-0
Library of Congress Cataloging-in-Publication Data on file.

Visit www.hyperionbooksforchildren.com

I'm a good boy.

Everybody says so.
Grandma says, "Paulie, you are as good as gold."

I thought I was pretty good, too,
until Prudence moved in next door.

Prudence is a **lunatic.**

Prudence walks her cat on a leash.
But mostly the cat walks on Prudence.
Grandma says, "Don't judge a book by its cover."

I'm giving Prudence one week to change my mind.

DAY 1 I Meet Prudence

I say, "I'm Paul. Welcome to the neighborhood."

"Hi, **Pill**!" Prudence says.

"I'm Paul," I say. "My dog's name is B

Prudence says, "I shall call your dog **Oops**. As in, '**Oops**, what a mistake giving that cute dog to you!'"

One day down, six to go.

DAY 2 I Meet the Cat

Prudence says, "My cat's name is Scratch.
Want to pet him?"
Just then, Scratch hisses and his hair stands up all over.
Prudence says, "I can tell Scratch likes you a lot."

Did I mention that Prudence is a **lunatic?**

DAY 3 Dumb: A Matter of Opinion

I say, "Prudence, look! See the string between our two windows? The boy who lived in your house and I used the string for sending secret messages. It's a cool invention."

Prudence says, "It's the **dumbest** thing I've ever seen!"

Well, the dumbest thing I've ever seen is a cat on a leash.

DAY 4 Eyes and Flies

The doorbell rings. It's Prudence.
She sticks her tongue out at me.
Then she says,

"Hello, FOUR EYES."

I tell Grandma about Prudence.
Grandma says, "You catch more flies with honey."
Sometimes I have no idea what Grandma's talking about.

Bobo and I have a talk in my room. He's a good listener.
He's the only one who understands.
Bobo thinks Prudence is a creep.

"That's mean," I say.
Bobo just stares at me.
Grandma would say that Bobo stood his ground.

DAY 5 Cooties

Prudence and I wait for the school bus.
I say, "May I stand under your umbrella, Prudence?"
Prudence says, "Ew! Stay away, **Cootie**!"

I say, "A cootie is actually an insect called a cockroach."
Prudence says, "Then you're a **cootie cockroach** with glasses."

Grandma always says, "Let a smile be your umbrella."
Grandma never waited for the bus with Prudence.

I tell Bobo, "I have a new name for Prudence.
I call her **PRUNEFACE.**"

Bobo thinks **PRUNEFACE** is a perfect name for her.
But I won't call her that to her face. I'm not mean.
I'll just keep it between Bobo and me.

DAY 6 A Froggy Day

I'm walking Bobo. Pruneface is walking Scratch.
Pruneface says, "**Oops** is so cute. You're cute too, **Pill** . . .
for a **frog**!"

I say, "Frogs are very important to our ecosystem, Prudence."
And I walk away.

I call her **PRUNEFACE**. But only in my head.
Bobo hears me.

THAT NIGHT

I dream I am a tiny dancing frog puppet.
Pruneface is pulling my strings.

I wake up. It's time to stop Pruneface.
Grandma would say, "Face your fears!"

TOMORROW I will talk to Pruneface.

UNLESS ANY OF THESE THINGS HAPPEN...

1. I get my own TALK SHOW.
2. Bobo and I go on the RUN.

3. The scary shrub
in our garden **EATS ME**.

4. I put on my baby sister's sweater
by **MISTAKE**, and it has to be
SURGICALLY REMOVED.

5. I'm **ARRESTED** when
Bobo **POOPS** on
Mr. Peeper's lawn
(again).

DAY 7 Time's Up

None of these things happen.

Bobo and I go to see Pruneface.
She is dressing Scratch in a pirate costume.

I say, "Please don't call me **PILL** anymore."
Pruneface says, "Okay, I'll call you **COOTIE COCKROACH FOUR-EYES FROGFACE PEAHEAD**!"

And I say,
"Why are you so mean, **PRUNEFACE?**"

Pruneface screams silently. Her mouth is a perfect O.
Then she runs inside her house.

I yell, "**FLIES EAT HONEY!**"
I have no idea what I'm talking about.

I feel bad all day. I stay in my room with Bobo.
I don't tell Mom or Dad or Grandma what I've done.
I brush my teeth, make my bed, and help Grandma fold the laundry.

"Paulie, you're as good as gold," Grandma says.

If she only knew.

THAT NIGHT

Bobo is barking. He sees a note clipped to the string outside my window! The note is in code.

DCMPF!!! EOD!!!!

What does it mean? I turn over the note and find out:

DON'T CALL ME PRUNEFACE!!!
END OF DISCUSSION!!!!

I write back.

DCBO!!!*
DCMP!!!**
DCMCCFEFFPH!!!***

Bobo doesn't like my note.
He thinks I used too many exclamation marks.

*Don't call Bobo Oops!!!
**Don't call me Pill!!!
***Don't call me cootie cockroach four-eyes frogface peahead!!!

THE NEXT MORNING

I wake up and look outside.
Bobo is playing fetch with Prudence.

How did that happen?

I call Bobo, and he comes running to me.
Prudence comes running, too.

She says, "I never liked dogs, but Bobo's the **coolest**.
Can I walk him, Paul?"

My grandma says you don't know
someone until you walk a mile in their shoes.

I have no idea what that means, but I let Prudence walk Bobo, and I walk Scratch. Prudence and I do not switch shoes. I won't wear pink sandals.